Ω

Published by
PEACHTREE PUBLISHERS, LTD.
1700 Chattahoochee Avenue
Atlanta, Georgia 30318-2112
www.peachtree-online.com

Text copyright © 2002 by Jeanne Willis
Illustrations copyright © 2002 by Susan Varley

First published in Great Britain in 2001 by Andersen Press Ltd.
under the title THE BOY WHO WAS BROUGHT UP BY TEDDY BEARS

Color separated in Switzerland by Photolitho AG, Zürich.
Printed and bound in Italy by Grafiche AZ, Verona.

10 9 8 7 6 5 4 3 2 1
First Edition

Cataloging-in-Publication Data is available from the Library of Congress

ISBN 1-56145-270-X

THE BOY WHO THOUGHT HE WAS A TEDDY BEAR

A fairy tale by **Jeanne Willis**

with pictures by **Susan Varley**

PEACHTREE
ATLANTA

Once there was a little boy who thought he was a Teddy Bear.
The fairies found him in the woods, in his carriage, when he was a baby.
They took him to their friends, the Three Bears,
who were having a picnic nearby.

"Where's his mother?" wondered Big Teddy.
"Where's his father?" wondered Middle Teddy.
"I can't see them anywhere!" said Little Teddy.
So, thinking the baby was all alone in the world,
they carried him back to their cottage.

When they got home, the baby began to cry.
"He's hungry. Let's give him some sawdust," said Big Teddy.
"He's thirsty. Let's give him some pondwater," said Middle Teddy.
"He's lonely. Let's give him a name," said Little Teddy.

They didn't know any People Names,
so they gave him Teddy Names instead.
"I shall call him Pinky, because he's pink," said Big Teddy.
"I shall call him Blinky, because he blinks," said Middle Teddy.
"And I shall call him Dinky," said Little Teddy,
"because he's so little."

The Teddy Bears weren't sure what to do with
the boy the fairies had found.

"I think we should take him to the police," said Big Teddy.
"I think we should take him to the doctor," said Middle Teddy.
"I think I should take him to bed with me," said Little Teddy.
Little Teddy got into bed and cuddled the baby.
The boy smiled and fell fast asleep.

The days turned into weeks,
the weeks turned into months,

and all this time the Three Bears
looked after Pinky Blinky Dinky.

He walked like a Teddy.
He growled like a Teddy.
He could even swivel his legs
all the way around...almost.

Grrrr

He slept in cupboards...

He sat on shelves...

He went to special picnics in the woods.

He even dressed like a Teddy
and tied a red ribbon round his neck
with an enormous bow in front.

And, of course, he was very cuddly.

Pinky Blinky Dinky truly believed
he was a Teddy Bear.
"We have to tell him the truth,"
said Big Teddy.
"It might upset him,"
said Middle Teddy.
"He'll find out soon enough,"
said Little Teddy.

And so he did.
One day there was a knock at the door.
It was Pinky's mother.

"I've been searching everywhere for my son," she said.
"The fairies brought me here."

"The fairies brought him to us," said Big Teddy.
"Because they thought he was lost," said Middle Teddy.
"But now he's found…" said Little Teddy.

And sure enough, there was Pinky Blinky Dinky,
lying with his legs in the air, upside down on the Teddy Bears' sofa!

"Edward!" cried his mother.
"My little boy!"
"What's a boy?" asked Pinky.
His mother tried to explain.

"But I don't want to be a boy!" he said.
"I want to be a Teddy Bear. I want to hide in cupboards
and go on picnics and play in the woods with my friends."
"Boys are allowed to do those things too," said his mother.
"But are boys allowed to have...cuddles?" he asked.
"Oh yes!" said his mother, and she gave him
the biggest bear hug he'd ever had.

"I wish I could have a hug like that," sighed Big Teddy.
"So do I," said Middle Teddy.
"Me too!" said Little Teddy.

"Come here then," said Mom.
And she cuddled every one of them all the way home.

To Owen & Kei –
K.G.

For Lori and Claire
E.B.

Text copyright © 2021 by Ken Geist
Illustrations copyright © 2021 by Eric Barclay

Printed in China 38 • First edition, April 2021 • Book design by Rae Crawford

There Was a
Silly Unicorn
Who Wanted to Fly

by Ken Geist   illustrated by Eric Barclay

Orchard Books · New York
An Imprint of Scholastic Inc.

There was a silly unicorn who wanted to fly.
I don't know why, but she wanted to fly.

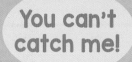

So she gave it a try.

There was a silly unicorn who wanted to fly.
She tried by swallowing a bee, OH MY!
The buzzing would surely make her go high.

Buzz!

Buzz!

Buzz!

Buzz!

I wish
I was still a
caterpillar!

There was a silly unicorn who wanted to fly.
A flapping butterfly was the thing to try.

She swallowed
the butterfly
to help the bee,

To flutter
and buzz
and dance
with the trees.

There was a silly unicorn
who wanted to fly.

Hey,
that's how
I sleep!

In swooped a bat,
she gulped with a sigh.

She swallowed the bat to help the butterfly,
Together they could float
and touch the sky.

There was a silly unicorn
who wanted to fly.
She gobbled up an owl with
one sleeping eye.

Who?
Me?

She swallowed the owl to help the bat,
All together they flapped and flapped.

There was a silly unicorn who wanted to fly.
She caught an eagle soaring by.

She swallowed the eagle to glide with the owl,
She swallowed the owl to wing with the bat,
She swallowed the bat to flap with the butterfly,
She swallowed the butterfly to buzz with the bee,

This unicorn was silly as silly can be!

There was a silly unicorn who wanted to fly.
She saw a rainbow in the bright blue sky.

Her hooves
began to rise . . .

twitched.

Her stomach

Higher

and higher,

much to her **surprise!**

She smiled and giggled
as she drifted up high,
And her magical horn tooted
a wonderful cry.

And all her friends were suddenly free . . .

To swirl and whirl and dance with the trees.